Dear Parents:

Congratulations! Your child is taking the first steps on an exciting journey. The destination? Independent reading!

STEP INTO READING® will help your child get there. The program offers five steps to reading success. Each step includes fun stories and colorful art or photographs. In addition to original fiction and books with favorite characters, there are Step into Reading Non-Fiction Readers, Phonics Readers and Boxed Sets, Sticker Readers, and Comic Readers—a complete literacy program with something to interest every child.

Learning to Read, Step by Step!

Ready to Read Preschool–Kindergarten
• big type and easy words • rhyme and rhythm • picture clues
For children who know the alphabet and are eager to begin reading.

Reading with Help Preschool–Grade 1
• basic vocabulary • short sentences • simple stories
For children who recognize familiar words and sound out new words with help.

Reading on Your Own Grades 1–3
• engaging characters • easy-to-follow plots • popular topics
For children who are ready to read on their own.

Reading Paragraphs Grades 2–3
• challenging vocabulary • short paragraphs • exciting stories
For newly independent readers who read simple sentences with confidence.

Ready for Chapters Grades 2–4
• chapters • longer paragraphs • full-color art
For children who want to take the plunge into chapter books but still like colorful pictures.

STEP INTO READING® is designed to give every child a successful reading experience. The grade levels are only guides; children will progress through the steps at their own speed, developing confidence in their reading.

Remember, a lifetime love of reading starts with a single step!

Visit us on the Web!
StepIntoReading.com
rhcbooks.com

Educators and librarians, for a variety of teaching tools, visit us at RHTeachersLibrarians.com

ISBN 978-0-593-17938-3 (trade)—ISBN 978-0-593-37534-1 (lib. bdg.)

Printed in the United States of America

10 9 8 7 6 5 4

nickelodeon

PAW PATROL™

SAVE THE DINOSAURS!

by Tex Huntley

illustrated by Nate Lovett

Random House 🏠 New York

The PAW Patrol
meets a new friend.
His name is Rex.
Rex lives in a land
filled with dinosaurs.

He asks the pups to visit.

The PAW Patrol gets a new truck!

The PAW Patrol and Rex
go for a ride.

They zoom through

a waterfall!

Welcome to Dino Land!

Oh, no!
Mayor Humdinger
followed the PAW Patrol!
He takes eggs
from different dinosaurs!

He wants his own

dinosaurs in Foggy Bottom.

Oh, no!
The mama brachiosaurus
is upset!

Rex can talk to dinosaurs.
He finds out that the
mama's egg is missing.

This is a job
for the PAW Patrol!

The pups find
Mayor Humdinger
with all the eggs.
They are hatching!

The baby brachiosaurus
runs away.

She is stuck on a cliff!

Skye to the rescue!

The mama
Tyrannosaurus rex
wants her baby back, too.

Rex's Dino Claw
saves the day!
Dino Land
is safe again.

Whenever you have
a dino-sized problem,
just yelp for help!